The Case Of The
Blue-Ribbon Horse™

The Case Of The
Blue-Ribbon Horse™

by I.K. Swobud

DUALSTAR PUBLICATIONS PARACHUTE PRESS

SCHOLASTIC INC.

New York   Toronto   London   Auckland   Sydney

DUALSTAR PUBLICATIONS **PARACHUTE PRESS**

Dualstar Publications
c/o Thorne and Company
1801 Century Park East
Los Angeles, CA 90067

Parachute Press
156 Fifth Avenue
Suite 325
New York, NY 10010

Published by Scholastic Inc.

With special thanks to Robert Thorne and Harold Weitzberg.

Printed in the U.S.A.
April 1998
ISBN: 0-590-29309-5
A B C D E F G H I J

1

A MYSTERY AT TEMPLETON STABLES

"Come on, Hot Chocolate," I whispered to the big horse. "Just picture a blue ribbon waiting for us on the other side of that jump!"

I know horses can't talk. But sometimes I feel as if Hot Chocolate understands every word I say.

Hot Chocolate gave a high whinny and trotted toward the low jump.

I tried to remember everything I'd learned in my riding classes. I leaned forward, put my weight in the stirrups, and held on tight with my knees.

Yay! Hot Chocolate and I soared over the jump and landed gently on the other side. A perfect jump!

I heard clapping and whistles from my own personal cheering section—that's my twin sister, Ashley, and my friend Tina Templeton.

"Way to go, Mary-Kate!" Tina cried.

I met Tina when I started taking riding lessons at the Templeton Stables last year. Her dad owns the stables and teaches a lot of the classes.

Tina is really cool. She's twelve—that's three years older than I am. She never treats me like a little kid—the way my big brother, Trent, does. And Trent and Tina are exactly the same age!

Tina knows everything about horses, even though she never rides them herself. I guess she knows so much because she's lived her whole life in a house that's right on the stable grounds. She's around horses every second of every day.

"Why don't you try taking the high jump?" Tina called.

"Hot Chocolate doesn't like the high ones," I reminded her.

I know Hot Chocolate better than anyone else does. I like to pretend he's my very own horse.

Most of the time I have to share him with the other kids who take lessons at the stables. But this whole week I'm the only one riding him. That's because I'm going to ride him in the big horse show on Saturday.

It's my very first show. And I'm really excited about it.

And here's something else that's really great. I'm off from school this week. It's spring vacation, so I can spend every day with Hot Chocolate!

"Come on," Tina called. "Try the high jump. You might be surprised."

"Okay," I answered. If Tina thought Hot

Chocolate was ready for the high jump, maybe he was.

I pushed my helmet farther down on my head. My stomach gave a little flip-flop when I looked over at the jump.

It was one straight rail in the middle of two posts. And it was much higher than the other jump.

I took a deep breath, then I turned Hot Chocolate toward the high jump. "Come on, Hot Chocolate. Let's do it," I said.

I gave Hot Chocolate a nudge with my heels. He trotted toward the rail. He picked up speed with every step. *Yes! He's going to do it!* I thought. *We're going to make it!*

The jump was coming up fast. I leaned forward. My legs tightened around his sides.

Suddenly, Hot Chocolate skidded to a stop.

"Ooof!" I grunted. I had to grab Hot Chocolate's mane with both hands to keep from falling off.

Ashley gave a loud gasp.

"Are you okay?" Tina yelled.

"Yes," I answered. "But I guess Hot Chocolate still isn't ready for the high jump."

"Don't give up on him too fast," Tina said.

"Do you mind moving out of the way?" I heard someone call from behind me.

I slowly looked over my shoulder—and saw Charlotte Taylor sitting on her horse, Magic.

Great, I thought. It figures that Charlotte would show up in time to see me and Hot Chocolate mess up.

Charlotte is my least favorite person at Templeton Stables. She is always bragging. She's always making fun of people. And lately she's also been playing mean tricks on me!

I clicked my tongue and gently pulled the reins to the left. I walked Hot Chocolate over to the side of the ring. "Ashley, come here for a second," I called.

Ashley ran up to me. Hot Chocolate poked his head over the fence and tried to stick his big nose in Ashley's pocket.

Ashley gave a squeak and jumped away. She's afraid of horses.

"Maybe Hot Chocolate thinks you are me," I said. "I always keep little treats for him in my pocket."

A lot of people mix me and Ashley up. We *are* alike on the outside. We both have strawberry blond hair and blue eyes. But on the inside we're completely different. For one thing, I love horses. Ashley's afraid of them.

I heard the sound of pounding hooves in the ring. I glanced over my shoulder and saw Magic racing for the high jump. He soared over with room to spare. Charlotte grinned at me and tossed her long black braid over her shoulder.

"That's her," I told Ashley. "That's Charlotte Taylor. She's the one I told you about. I know she's been playing mean tricks on me. And I want you to help me prove it."

Ashley pulled out her notebook, the notebook she always uses when we're on a case.

Ashley and I are detectives. We run the Olsen and Olsen Mystery Agency out of the attic of our house. But this would be the first time an Olsen hired Olsen and Olsen to solve a mystery!

2

MARY-KATE NEEDS HELP

"**I** promised I'd help you," Ashley said. "But I have to treat this like any other case. That means thinking about all the possible suspects—not just Charlotte. I have to keep an open mind, like Great-grandma Olive taught us."

Great-grandma Olive is the reason Ashley and I became detectives. She read us so many great mystery stories that we decided we wanted to solve mysteries ourselves.

"Okay, I want to make sure I have all the

facts," Ashley said. "First your whatchamacall-it—the thing you steer with—was in the wrong place, right?"

"Hot Chocolate's bridle," I told her. "When I got to the barn Monday morning, someone had moved the bridle from the tack room—that's the place where all the saddles and bridles are kept. It took me so long to find it, I was late to class."

Ashley wrote this information in her notebook.

"Then, on Tuesday morning, Hot Chocolate's blanket was missing," I said.

Ashley wrote as fast as she could to keep up with me.

"This morning, Hot Chocolate's feet were all muddy, and I know I cleaned them before I went home yesterday," I continued.

"Anything else?" Ashley asked.

"Isn't that enough?" I demanded. "We should be able to solve this mystery in two seconds. Charlotte is the only one around here who is mean enough to play those tricks on me."

Ashley shook her head. "I really don't think there is a mystery here at all," she said. "The only mystery around here is why *you* think there is a mystery."

Hot Chocolate gave a loud snort.

"Even Hot Chocolate thinks that's silly," I said. "Of course there is a mystery."

"Well, you're always losing things at home. And your stuff is always ending up on my side of our room," Ashley pointed out. "Are you sure you didn't just forget where you left Hot Chocolate's bridle and saddle blanket?"

"I'm positive," I answered. "Besides, what about Hot Chocolate's dirty feet? How do you explain that?"

"Hmm," Ashley answered. "I'm not sure."

"Well, *I'm* sure," I said. "Charlotte is playing tricks on me!"

"Do you really think Charlotte is that mean?" Ashley asked.

"Yes, I do," I replied.

Charlotte took Magic over the high jump again. She gave Ashley and me a big, big smile.

I knew it was totally fake.

Charlotte trotted Magic up next to me and Hot Chocolate. Ashley took three big steps back—even though the ring fence was between her and Charlotte's horse.

"What's the matter?" Charlotte asked. "Are you afraid of horses or something?"

"A little," Ashley admitted.

Charlotte laughed. "Mary-Kate is the one who should be afraid," she said. "Anyone who rides as badly as she does should be terrified to get near a horse."

Charlotte turned Magic around. She took him over the high jump again.

"Now do you think she's mean enough to play those tricks?" I whispered to Ashley.

"Hmm," Ashley said. She stared at Charlotte. "Maybe there *is* a mystery here to solve."

3

Ashley Has A Plan

"Okay, I'll put Charlotte down as a suspect," Ashley said, as I led Hot Chocolate into the barn.

"Yes! Now all we need is proof that she's guilty," I answered.

"Not so fast," Ashley said. "What we need is an investigation."

Ashley sat down on a bale of hay near Hot Chocolate's stall. "I'm going to make notes of exactly where you put all Hot Chocolate's things and how he looks when you're finished for the day," she said. "That way when we come to the stables tomorrow morning we'll know for sure if anything is different."

"Good idea," I answered. I opened the door of Hot Chocolate's stall, and he trotted inside.

"First I have to take off Hot Chocolate's saddle, and wipe him down with a dry cloth," I explained. "Then I have to brush him. And make sure there are no tangles in his mane and tail. And clean his hooves. And then I have to oil his saddle."

Hot Chocolate gave a loud snort.

"And I have to feed him," I said quickly. I gave Hot Chocolate a pat on the nose. "Don't worry," I told the big horse. "I would never forget to give you your oats and your water and your special apple-and-carrot salad."

"Whoa!" Ashley exclaimed. "All that work to get on a horse?"

"You have to know how to take good care of your equipment and your horse or you can't be a good rider. That's what Mr. Templeton always says," I told her.

Kenny Kendricks wandered by carrying the big pitchfork he uses to throw clean hay into the horses' stalls. Kenny is in college. He works at the stables part-time. "Hey, Hot Chocolate," Kenny said. "Did I get your stall clean enough for you? You know you're my favorite, right?"

I giggled. Kenny calls every horse at the stables his favorite.

"You're doing a great job taking care of him, Mary-Kate," Kenny said.

"Thanks," I answered. "I'm assistant stable manager this month. That means I have to set an extra good example for everyone."

Every month Mr. Templeton picks one of his students to be assistant stable manager and help him out around the barn. This month it was my turn—my first turn.

Kenny nodded. Then he made his way down to the last stall in the row. "How's my favorite horse today?" I heard him ask.

I ran my fingers over the white spots on Hot Chocolate's back. I call the spots Hot Chocolate's marshmallows. Then I gently slid Hot Chocolate's bridle over his ears and slipped it out of his mouth. "I love taking care of Hot Chocolate," I told Ashley. "It makes me feel like he's really my very own horse."

Someone gave a loud, long laugh behind me.

A loud, long, *mean* laugh.

I spun around—and saw Charlotte leading Magic into the barn.

"And you've been taking really good care of *your* horse," Charlotte taunted. "You lost his bridle and his saddle blanket. Next you'll probably lose Hot Chocolate himself. I doubt you'll ever get to be assistant stable manager again."

Before I could answer, the barn door swung open—and Mr. Templeton hurried inside.

"Hi, girls," he called. "Have you seen my riding helmet around? I'm getting ready to teach a jumping class, and I can't find it."

I tried not to giggle. "Um, it's on your head," I told him.

"Oops! No wonder I didn't see it anywhere. Tina is always giving me a hard time for being so forgetful," he said.

"You're just like Mary-Kate." Charlotte smirked at me. "She's always losing things too."

Mr. Templeton frowned. "What do you mean?" he asked Charlotte.

"Mr. Templeton, remember your class is waiting," I said quickly. I didn't want Charlotte to tell him about the missing bridle and saddle blanket. I didn't want him to think I was doing a bad job with Hot Chocolate.

"My class! I almost forgot!" Mr. Templeton spun around and headed for the door.

"Hey, Mr. Templeton. I taught Magic a new trick. Let me show it to you," Charlotte called.

"I can't right now," Mr. Templeton said. "Maybe later."

He rushed out the door.

"Maybe the whole class wants to see Magic's trick!" Charlotte hurried after Mr. Templeton, leading Magic behind her.

When she reached the door, she turned around and faced me. "Assistant stable managers don't treat their horses the way you do, Mary-Kate. You'd better shape up."

Charlotte swung onto Magic's back and trotted out of the barn.

Ashley shook her head. "She really doesn't like you, does she?"

"So you believe me now, right?" I asked. "Charlotte has been playing mean tricks on me and Hot Chocolate."

"I'm still not sure," Ashley said slowly. "But I have a plan to find out."

4

STAKEOUT SURPRISE

"**Y**ou were right, Ashley. The hayloft is the perfect place for a stakeout!" I whispered.

"I told you I had a plan," Ashley whispered back. She lay stretched out in the hay a few feet away from me.

Ashley came up with the idea for us to get to the stable really, really early the next day and hide in the hayloft. That way we could catch whoever was playing those mean tricks in the act.

Stakeouts are my least favorite part of

being a detective. It's so boring sitting in one place and waiting for something to happen.

"I just wish it wasn't so dark up here," I said. "It's a little spooky."

"I don't think it's spooky—I think it's itchy," Ashley complained. "Pieces of hay keep jabbing into me."

"I know. But if you stay still, the hay doesn't itch so much," I answered. "Now, be quiet. Our plan won't work if anyone knows we're up in the hayloft."

"I hope we don't have to wait too much longer," Ashley whispered. "It smells icky in here."

"It doesn't smell icky. It smells like horses," I said. "Now, shhh!"

"Well, horses smell icky, Mary-Kate," Ashley answered.

Squeeeek.

I grabbed Ashley's arm. "That's the barn door," I whispered.

I peered down into the barn. From up here

I could see Hot Chocolate's back—shiny brown with white marshmallows.

I heard footsteps moving toward him. But whoever was down there was walking *under* the hayloft—and I couldn't see them.

Thump, thump, thump. I heard the sound of boots on the barn floor. Moving closer and closer to Hot Chocolate's stall.

Come on, I thought. Come out where we can see you.

I inched a little closer to the edge of the hayloft. A piece of hay brushed against my nose.

My nose began to itch.

Oh, no! I felt a sneeze coming on. A big one.

I couldn't sneeze now. It would scare away whoever was down there in the barn.

I tried not to think about my itchy nose. But it didn't help.

"Ah-ah-ah…"

My sneeze was starting!

And it was too strong to be stopped.

"Ah-choo!"

I froze.

Thump. Thump. Thump.

I heard the boots moving away from Hot Chocolate's stall.

"Oh, no!" I whispered. "They're getting away!"

"Come on!" Ashley answered.

We darted across the loft to the ladder.

"Look!" Ashley gasped.

We both stared as the ladder began to move.

"Stop!" Ashley yelled.

But whoever was down there didn't stop. They gave the ladder a jerk. Then I heard it crash to the floor.

I stared over at Ashley. "We're trapped up here!"

5

HORSES, HORSES, AND MORE HORSES

The barn door slammed shut.

"I can't believe it!" I cried. "We almost caught Charlotte—and she got away!"

"Mary-Kate, for the billionth time, we don't know if it was Charlotte," Ashley said.

I rolled my eyes.

"The most important thing is how are we going to get down?" Ashley asked.

"It's way too far to jump," I answered. "I guess there's only one thing we can do."

"What?" Ashley demanded.

"Scream." I cupped my hands around my mouth and screamed as loud as I could. "Hellllp!"

"Help! Help! Help!" Ashley shouted.

The barn door flew open.

Tina ran into the barn. Her brown eyes opened wide as she stared into the hayloft. "What are you doing up there?" she asked.

"We got here early, and we thought the hayloft would be a fun place to wait for class to start," I said.

It's better not to tell anyone you're on a stakeout—even friends like Tina.

"Then the ladder fell down—and now we're stuck," Ashley added.

"You must be very happy to see me," Tina teased. She gave a grunt as she dragged the ladder back over to the hayloft.

"Very, very happy," Ashley said. She scrambled down the ladder. I was right behind her.

"Do you want to come up to the house for some hot chocolate?" Tina asked. "The kind you drink, I mean."

"Thanks," I said. Ashley and I followed her out of the barn.

We walked past the ring. Andrea, one of the riding teachers, was exercising Mr. Wiggins. Mr. Wiggins is the horse the littlest kids ride. He moves really slowly.

I didn't see anyone else. Whoever had been sneaking around in the barn was gone.

Ashley grabbed my arm. "Don't worry. We'll do another stakeout tomorrow," she whispered in my ear.

I nodded. When Olsen and Olsen are on a case, nothing stops us, I thought.

We climbed the steps up to Tina's big front porch. Sam, one of the kids in my riding class, sat in the rocking chair near the door.

"My mom dropped me off early because she had a big meeting or something," Sam said.

"Come on in," Tina answered. "Don't tell Dad I was outside, okay?" she asked all of us. "I have a cold and he made me promise to stay in the house today. He's such a worrywart."

Mr. Templeton *is* a worrywart. He's always giving us lectures on riding safety.

"We won't tell," Ashley promised.

Sam nodded.

Tina led us down a long hall to the kitchen. Ashley, Sam, and I sat at the kitchen table while Tina pulled packages of instant hot chocolate out of the cupboard.

I couldn't stop staring around the room. There were horses everywhere! There were horse magnets on the refrigerator. A cloth with a big horse embroidered on it was spread on the table. Horses pranced across the curtains hanging in the windows. There were even horses on the cups Tina made our hot chocolate in.

Tina handed Ashley, Sam, and me our drinks. "Let's drink this in the living room."

I took a sip of my drink as I followed Tina back down the hall and into the living room. My eyes widened as I sat down on the sofa.

The living room had even more horses than the kitchen!

The material covering the couch and the chairs had horses on it. The rug in front of the fireplace had horses on it.

There were pictures of horses on the walls. Every book in the bookcase was about horses. And the view from the big front window was of the ring!

"Uh-oh. Your house is going to make Ashley nervous," I teased.

Tina looked confused.

"Ashley is sort of afraid of horses," I explained.

"Really?" Sam asked. "Even Hot Chocolate? He's the nicest horse at the stables."

"Pictures of horses don't bother me," Ashley said. "But the real ones are just too big. Especially their feet. And their teeth."

"That's true," Tina agreed. "But just because an animal is big doesn't mean it's dangerous. Think about Hot Chocolate. He's really big—

but he's really sweet too, just like Sam said. He would never hurt anybody."

Tina set her cup on the coffee table. "And my aunt's dog is really little—but he's really mean. He tries to bite anybody who comes near him. His teeth are really small—but that doesn't mean they don't hurt!"

Ashley nodded slowly. "I never thought about it that way." She smiled at Tina. "I'm surprised you don't ride. You sound like you really love horses."

"I do love them," Tina answered. "But it takes a lot of time to be a good rider. And I'm in Girl Scouts. And I'm taking violin lessons. I...I just don't have time to ride, too."

"I guess your dad doesn't have time to do anything else," I said. "Did he win all those?" I pointed to the row of shining trophies and blue ribbons on the mantel.

"Yeah," Tina said quickly. "He's an amazing rider."

I stood up and headed for the mantel. I

reached for one of the trophies, so I could take a closer look.

"No!" Tina cried.

I jerked my hand away and hurried back to the sofa.

"I'm sorry," Tina said. "I didn't mean to scare you. My dad doesn't let anyone touch his trophies. You know what a worrywart he is. I guess he's afraid they'll get broken or something."

"I guess if Hot Chocolate and I won a prize I would be really careful with it too," I said.

I smiled as I imagined myself accepting a beautiful trophy or a blue ribbon at the horse show on Saturday.

It could happen, I told myself. I take good care of Hot Chocolate, and he takes care of me. We make a winning team!

"Mary-Kate, wake up, it's starting to get light out!" Ashley exclaimed.

I sat up in bed and frowned at Ashley. "Why

did you wake me up? I was dreaming I was in the horse show. Hot Chocolate had a pair of beautiful marshmallow wings, and we were flying over every jump. And some of them were as tall as our house!"

I stretched back out in bed and pulled my pillow over my head. "Now leave me alone and let me finish my dream."

Ashley snatched the pillow away. "We have to get to the stables for our stakeout."

"Right!" I exclaimed. "Today we are going to catch Charlotte—no matter what!"

I threw off the covers and jumped out of bed. I yanked on a pair of jeans and my favorite red sweatshirt. Then I pulled on a pair of matching red socks.

Now all I needed were my riding boots. I reached under my bed—but all I felt was a little dust.

"Have you seen my boots, Ashley?" I asked.

"No. I told you you're always losing stuff," Ashley said. Her voice sounded muffled because she was talking while she pulled her sweater over her head.

"Just help me find them, okay?" I answered. "We're going to be late. And if we're late, we won't be able to catch Charlotte playing one of her mean tricks."

Ashley gave a big sigh. "Mary-Kate, we still don't know for sure that Charlotte is the one playing those tricks. Repeat after me—detectives have to keep an open mind."

"Okay, okay," I muttered.

Our six-year-old sister, Lizzie, wandered into our room. She had a polka-dot scarf tied over her head and one of Mom's clip-on earrings on one ear.

"Lizzie, it's not anywhere near Halloween!" I exclaimed. "Why are you dressed up like a pirate?

"Do you see my shoes around anywhere?" I asked before Lizzie could answer.

"Or mine," Ashley added. "I can't find my shoes either!"

"I'm searching for treasure," Lizzie said.

I ignored her. Usually I think it's fun to play with Lizzie. But right then all I wanted to do was get to the stables.

"Ashley, your shoes are missing, too?" I cried.

"Every single pair," she answered. She pointed to the shoe rack on the inside of her closet door. It was absolutely empty. Even Ashley's pink ballet slippers were gone!

"Doesn't anyone want to help me look for treasure?" Lizzie pouted.

Ashley turned around and stared at her. "What kind of treasure?" she asked.

"Jewels, and gold coins and…shoes!" Lizzie answered.

"I can't believe Lizzie hid our shoes," I complained as we biked to the stables. "She ruined our stakeout. We're so late that I'm barely going to make it to class on time."

"We can't give up. We'll have to try again

tomorrow," Ashley said.

We parked our bikes in front of the barn and rushed inside.

"Don't worry, Hot Chocolate. I'm here," I called. I raced over to his stall. "Oh, no!" I cried. "Oh, no! Oh, no! Oh, no!"

"What's wrong?" Ashley exclaimed.

All I could do was point at Hot Chocolate's stall.

It was empty!

6

WHERE, OH WHERE, CAN MY LITTLE HORSE BE?

"**S**omeone stole Hot Chocolate!" I cried.

"Maybe one of the other students took him out," Ashley said.

"I'm the only one riding him this whole week, remember?" I asked. "We have to go look for him!"

"Lose something, Mary-Kate?" Charlotte asked as she led Magic out of his stall.

I glared at her. She stole Hot Chocolate. I knew it. This was her meanest trick ever!

"Come on, Mary-Kate," Ashley said. "The

most important thing right now is finding Hot Chocolate."

Ashley was right. I would figure out what to do about Charlotte later.

Hot Chocolate could be scared. He could be hurt. He needed me.

"Let's go!" I cried. Ashley and I raced toward the barn door.

"I hope you find him before the horse show on Saturday," Charlotte called after us.

First we checked the riding ring. No Hot Chocolate.

Then we checked the big pasture where the horses graze on nice days. No Hot Chocolate.

"Charlotte has gone too far!" I exclaimed.

"I'm still not sure Charlotte did this," Ashley said. "But I *am* sure of one thing—we absolutely, positively have a mystery. Even you couldn't misplace a whole horse!"

"Of course Charlotte did this!" I exclaimed. "Remember what she said the other day? She said that I lost Hot Chocolate's bridle and his saddle blanket, and that next I would lose Hot Chocolate himself."

"It does look like she's the one," Ashley agreed. She flipped through her notebook. "But let's think about the other people at the stables. So far I've met Sam, Kenny, and Tina. Then there is Andrea and Mr. Templeton."

I knew Ashley was right. A good detective considers all the possibilities.

I slowly shook my head. "I can't think of a motive for any of them," I said.

Motive is one of the words Great-grandma Olive taught us. It means the reason a person commits a crime.

"And Charlotte does have a motive. I think she's jealous that you are assistant stable manager," Ashley said. "But we need proof before we can be sure she's the one. Getting proof is the only way we're going to stop her from playing those mean tricks on you."

"I guess we should go find Mr. Templeton and tell him Hot Chocolate is missing," I said. I sighed as Ashley and I trudged back toward the ring.

"I feel really bad," I told Ashley. "I'm supposed to be taking care of Hot Chocolate. What is Mr. Templeton going to think when I tell him I lost my horse?"

"It wasn't your fault, Mary-Kate," Ashley said. "Don't feel bad."

I tried to smile at her. "I know, but—"

I heard a long, high whinny.

A whinny I recognized.

"Hot Chocolate!" I yelled.

I heard the whinny again. I raced toward the sound. Ashley was right behind me.

I spotted Hot Chocolate tied to a tree near the Templetons' back porch. I ran straight up to him and gave him a big hug.

"You're okay now," I said. I kissed him on his soft nose.

Ashley didn't get close enough to Hot Chocolate to kiss him. But she did give him a big smile.

"Don't worry," Ashley told Hot Chocolate. "Olsen and Olsen are going to find out who stole you and tied you up out here. We promise."

I rode Hot Chocolate through one of the pastures to get him warmed up, then I trotted him over to the ring. Tina swung open the gate for me.

"Sorry I'm late," I called to Andrea. She was teaching that day's riding class.

"That's okay," Andrea answered. "Just get in line behind Charlotte. We're practicing jumps."

I nudged Hot Chocolate with my heels and guided him to his place behind Magic.

"The assistant stable manager is supposed to set a good example for everyone," Charlotte said softly. "Being late is a *bad* example, Mary-Kate."

"Okay, Sam," Andrea called. "Take whichever jump you want—the high one or the low one. What I'm interested in is your form. Keep your knees pressed in, your heels down, and your shoulders back."

Sam took his horse over the low jump. "Perfect," Andrea called.

"That's what we have to do, Hot Chocolate," I whispered.

I watched each of the seven other kids in my class take one of the jumps. Mr. Templeton always says you can learn a lot from watching other people—what they do right, and their mistakes too.

When it was Charlotte's turn, she took Magic over the high jump—of course.

Before Andrea could call my name, Hot Chocolate started running. He chased after Magic—heading straight for the high jump!

"Hot Chocolate, what are you doing?" I cried. I tried to steer him toward the low jump. But he wouldn't go.

He raced straight for the high jump.

Oh, no! Were we going to make it?

HOT CHOCOLATE TAKES A BOW

"You can do it, Hot Chocolate! You can do it!" I cried.

I leaned forward and squeezed with my knees.

Then we were in the air. I felt like I was back in my dream—riding a flying horse.

"Good job!" Andrea exclaimed when Hot Chocolate landed. "But next time wait until I call your name."

"I will," I answered. "We'll both wait next time, right, Hot Chocolate?" I whispered. One of his ears twitched, so I figured he was listening to me.

Ashley gave me a thumbs-up as I rode past.

"I told you Hot Chocolate could do it!" Tina exclaimed.

Charlotte trotted up to me and shook her head. "That's nothing," she said. "Watch this."

She patted Magic twice on the neck—and Magic gave a low bow, stretching one of his legs out in front of him.

"Wow," I mumbled. Magic's trick *was* pretty cool.

"Betcha Hot Chocolate can't do *that*," Charlotte taunted.

"So what if he can't?" I asked. "He's still the best horse around." I gave Hot Chocolate two pats on the neck.

Then I felt myself sinking to the ground. What was happening?

Hot Chocolate lowered himself in a deep bow—exactly like the one Magic just did!

* * *

"Maybe it was *monkey see—monkey do*," Ashley said that night. "Hot Chocolate saw Magic go over the high jump and do that bow—so he did them too."

"Ooo-ooo-ooo!" Lizzie bounced up and down on Ashley's bed and made monkey sounds.

"Hot Chocolate is a horse, not a monkey," I answered. "Horses don't learn by watching other horses."

I sat behind Ashley on my bed. She was letting me braid her hair. I wanted to practice braiding, because I planned to braid Hot Chocolate's mane for the horse show.

A person's hair and a horse's mane are pretty different. But I figured any practice would help.

"Besides," I continued, "Hot Chocolate has seen the other horses go over the high jump a bunch of times—but he would never go near the jump until today. And there is no way he could have learned that bow just by watching

Magic. Someone taught him how to do it—and it wasn't me."

Ashley reached for her notebook.

"You've got to hold still or your braid is going to come out all crooked," I told her.

"I still don't see why you want to braid Hot Chocolate's mane," Lizzie said. "Hot Chocolate is a boy, right?"

"In big horse shows *all* the horses wear braids," I explained. "I want Hot Chocolate to feel like one of those horses. I want him to feel like a winner."

"Okay, so someone has been teaching Hot Chocolate," Ashley said. "But who? And why? You're the only one riding him this whole week."

I tied a purple ribbon at the bottom of Ashley's braid. I thought the braid looked pretty good. But not good enough for Hot Chocolate.

I untied the ribbon and unbraided Ashley's hair so I could try again.

"I don't know," I admitted. "I thought Charlotte was playing those tricks on me and Hot Chocolate. But she would never do something nice—like teach Hot Chocolate how to bow. This is weird—really weird."

Ashley sighed. "Ouch. My head hurts. Either you're braiding my hair too tight, or this case is too hard."

"I think this is Olsen and Olsen's toughest case yet!" I agreed.

8

TOO LATE

“**W**e'll definitely be at the stables early enough for our stakeout this morning," I whispered. I didn't want to wake up Mom or Dad or Lizzie or Trent.

"Yeah," Ashley whispered back. She swung the front door open and we tiptoed out.

"And this time we won't hide anyplace that has a ladder," I said. "Charlotte won't be able to trap us again! We will definitely catch her today!"

This time Ashley didn't even bother to

The New Adventures of Mary-Kate & Ashley™

DETECTIVE TRICK

COLLECTING FINGERPRINTS

What you'll need:

Charcoal Powder
(make by scraping sandpaper
over a piece of charcoal)
Talcum Powder

Clear Tape
Artist's Paintbrush
Light-colored Paper
Dark-colored Paper

The best surfaces to lift fingerprints from are metal, glass, plastic, and paper. First, sprinkle some powder on the print (use black powder for prints on light-colored surfaces, and white powder for prints on dark surfaces). Take your paintbrush and gently brush the powder over the print. Blow away the extra powder. Then place a piece of tape, sticky side down, over the print. Rub your fingernail over the tape to make sure you pick up all the powder. Pull up the tape—and the print comes with it! Now stick the tape on a piece of paper (use light-colored paper when you use black powder, and dark-colored paper when you use white powder) and you're ready to study the print.

From
The Case Of The Blue-Ribbon Horse

The New Adventures of Mary-Kate & Ashley™

DETECTIVE TRICK

WORD SPACE CODE

Here's an easy way to write a secret message. Just move the space between the words so the words no longer make sense.

In this code, the words "Detectives at Work" could look like this:

DET E
CTI VESA
TWO
RK

From our next mystery...
The Case Of The Haunted Camp

remind me to keep an open mind.

We grabbed our bikes out of the garage and hopped on. Then we took off for the stables. We pedaled so hard, I was out of breath after three blocks. But I didn't slow down.

I kept pumping on the pedals until we reached the stables. We hid our bikes behind the shrubs alongside the barn so no one would realize we were around. A stakeout doesn't really work if other people *know* you are on a stakeout.

"I want to check Hot Chocolate before we get in our hiding place," I said as we hurried into the barn.

Thump, thump, thump.

I heard footsteps. Someone was running through the barn! "They are getting away!" I yelled.

I raced over to Hot Chocolate's stall. I stared inside and gasped.

"Who's there?" Ashley demanded.

"No one," I answered. "But someone left a

saddle on Hot Chocolate!"

"Even I know you're not supposed to leave the saddle on," Ashley said.

I ran my hand over the black saddle's soft leather. Then I felt something cool and hard under my fingers. I looked down and saw a shiny brass nameplate with two letters engraved on it.

A huge grin broke across my face. "Ashley, We just got our best clue yet!"

OUR VERY BEST CLUE

"**T**his saddle has initials on it," I told Ashley.

She pulled out her notebook. "What are they?"

"CT!" I cried. "That has to stand for Charlotte Taylor. I bet she was about to take Hot Chocolate out of the barn. Then she heard us coming and ran off."

Ashley nibbled the end of her pencil as she flipped through the pages of the notebook.

"There's one problem, Mary-Kate," she said.

"I made some notes about Charlotte's riding equipment, and Charlotte has a brown saddle. The saddle on Hot Chocolate is black."

I plopped down on a bale of hay. I thought we finally had a great clue—and it turned out to be as confusing as everything else about this case!

"Well…maybe Charlotte has two saddles," I said. "Yeah! That's it. Charlotte has the most fancy equipment of anyone at the stables. She has special horse treats for Magic. And a hand-woven saddle blanket. It would be just like Charlotte to—"

"To what?"

I jerked my head around and saw Charlotte standing in the doorway of the barn. She put her hands on her hips. "It would be just like me to what, Mary-Kate?"

I jumped up and marched over to Charlotte. "It would be just like you to play mean tricks on me and Hot Chocolate," I said.

"Mary-Kate, wait," Ashley called. "We don't

have proof."

I ignored Ashley. "I know you hid his bridle and his saddle blanket," I told Charlotte. "And I know you took him out of his stall and tied him up by the Templetons' house so I couldn't find him. And I know you planned to ride him someplace this morning."

"Are you crazy? Why would I want to ride Hot Chocolate when I have Magic? Magic's a hundred times better than your stupid horse," Charlotte snapped.

"I don't know why you'd want to ride Hot Chocolate," I shot back. "But I do know that you put your saddle on him, and—"

Charlotte stomped past me and over to Hot Chocolate's stall. "That's not my saddle," she announced. "Look at the way the leather cracks on the side. It's obviously not the best. I would never own a saddle like that."

"Don't try to lie about it," I said. "The saddle has your initials on it."

"They may be my initials, but that is *not* my

saddle," Charlotte said. Then she turned around and swept out of the barn without another word.

I turned to Ashley. "Can you believe she lied to us like that?"

"I'm not sure she is lying," Ashley said. We need more facts, Mary-Kate. You have to stop jumping to conclusions."

I snapped my fingers. "I know—we can get fingerprints." I opened the door to Hot Chocolate's stall and stepped inside.

"How can you get fingerprints off a horse?" Ashley asked.

"Not off Hot Chocolate—off the saddle!" I answered.

"Great idea," Ashley said. She opened her backpack and pulled out our fingerprint kit.

I unsaddled Hot Chocolate. I tried not to get too many of my own fingerprints on the saddle.

Then I carried the saddle to the tack room at one end of the barn. Ashley followed close behind me. I hung the saddle on one of the wooden posts sticking out from the back wall.

Ashley unscrewed the jar of white talcum powder we use to collect fingerprints. "Where should I put the powder?" she asked.

"Try the leather strip of one of the stirrups," I answered. "When you saddle a horse you usually touch that part of the saddle. And I made sure not to touch it when I carried the saddle in here."

I carefully lifted up one of the leather strips. Ashley used a small paintbrush to spread the talcum powder over the leather.

Then she blew across the powder. Some of it flew off. But some of it stayed stuck to the leather of the stirrup.

The places where the powder stayed stuck were the places with fingerprints. Now all we had to do was get those fingerprints off the leather.

Ashley laid pieces of tape across the patches of white powder. Then she pulled off the tape—with the powder stuck to it—and spread the tape on a clean sheet of black paper.

Now we could see the fingerprints outlined in powder against the dark paper.

"Good job," I told Ashley.

"Our fingerprint kit worked great," she agreed. "But I just realized we have a really big problem!"

10

THE TROUBLE WITH CHARLOTTE

"**W**hat?" I exclaimed. "What big problem do we have?"

"We have fingerprints from the saddle. But whose fingerprints are we going to compare those fingerprints to?" Ashley asked.

Oh, no! We needed to find the fingerprints that matched the fingerprints from the saddle. That was the only way to find out who put the saddle on Hot Chocolate.

"Okay, let's get Charlotte's fingerprints," I said.

"Right!" Ashley said. "And if we get her fingerprints and they don't match, we'll know more than we do now. We'll know that Charlotte *isn't* the person we're looking for."

"Her fingerprints will match," I said. "I know it. I know she was lying when she said this saddle wasn't hers."

Ashley grinned at me. "There's one way to find out—so let's go!"

"Um, Charlotte, um, I wanted to tell you I'm sorry," I said as soon as our daily riding class was over, and we were back in the barn.

Charlotte looked up from grooming Magic. Her mouth dropped open. She stared at me as if she couldn't believe what she was hearing.

I couldn't believe what I was *saying*. But it was all part of the plan Ashley and I came up with to get Charlotte's fingerprints.

"I shouldn't have accused you of playing mean tricks on me and Hot Chocolate," I continued. "And I should have believed you when you told me the saddle I found on Hot Chocolate wasn't yours."

"That's right, you should have," Charlotte answered.

I forced myself to smile at her. It made my face hurt.

"I brought you some water," I said. "I always get really thirsty after our class, and I thought you might too."

I held out a paper cup filled with water. I was careful only to let the very tips of my fingers touch it. We wanted Charlotte's fingerprints—not mine!

Charlotte gave a little sniff. "No thanks, Mary-Kate," she said. "I drink only mineral water that comes all the way from France. It's the very best."

"Oh." I didn't know what else to say. I trudged out of the barn and over to the picnic table near the ring. I sat down across from Ashley.

"Give me the cup, and I'll dust it for fingerprints," she said. She reached out her hand.

"Forget it," I answered. "Charlotte drinks only special mineral water—from France. She wouldn't even touch the cup. I was nice to her for nothing!"

"Okay, we need Plan B," Ashley said. "Where else can we get Charlotte's fingerprints?"

That's one great thing about Ashley. She never gives up.

"I know! Her saddle!" Ashley cried.

"Huh? We already got fingerprints from her saddle," I said.

"Not the saddle that was on Hot Chocolate. The brown saddle that Charlotte uses in class," Ashley explained.

"Let's go!" I exclaimed. I pulled Ashley to her feet, and we ran straight to the barn and down to the tack room. That's where all the saddles are kept.

We burst through the door. Charlotte sat on one of the benches.

"What are you doing?" I yelled.

Charlotte raised her eyebrows. "What does it look like I'm doing? I'm oiling my saddle." She held up the bottle of oil so Ashley and I could see it. "This oil comes all the way from Italy. It's the very best."

Charlotte placed a few more drops of oil on her cloth. Then she rubbed the cloth over the seat of the saddle and down the stirrups.

Rubbing away her fingerprints!

"Come on, Mary-Kate," Ashley muttered. She led the way back outside to the picnic table.

I slammed my fists down on the table. "We're never going to get Charlotte's fingerprints!"

"Time to think of Plan C," Ashley said, her voice calm.

"I hope we don't have to go through the whole alphabet," I moaned.

"We won't," Ashley said firmly. "I'm sure our next plan will work. All we have to do is think of another way to get Charlotte's finger-prints."

Okay, think, I told myself. I closed my eyes and tried to picture everything in the barn. What did Charlotte touch—that a million other people didn't touch, too?

The best surfaces to get fingerprints from are glass, plastic, metal, and paper. But other surfaces work too—like wood!

"The door of Magic's stall!" I burst out. "Charlotte opens the door to Magic's stall every time she takes him out to ride, and every time she puts him back."

Ashley's eyes started to sparkle. "Let's go!" she cried.

We raced back to the barn and barreled through the door.

I stopped so suddenly that Ashley crashed into me.

Charlotte knelt in front of Magic's stall door.

"What are you doing now?" I shouted.

Charlotte shook her head. "What does it look like I'm doing?" she asked. "I'm polishing the door to Magic's stall."

She held up the bottle of furniture polish so Ashley and I could see it. "This polish comes all the way from Denmark. It's the very best," she said.

Charlotte sprayed some polish onto the stall door and rubbed it with a checkered cloth.

Rubbing away her fingerprints!

SOMETHING IS WRONG

"**I**f Plan D doesn't work, I'm going to scream," I told Ashley.

I plopped down next to her on a bale of hay in the corner of the barn.

"Would you calm down, Mary-Kate? We still have twenty-two letters left in the alphabet," Ashley answered.

"Don't even say that!" I exclaimed.

Sometimes I hate it when Ashley is so calm and logical!

She held up both hands. "Sorry."

The barn door swung open. "Get ready. Here comes Charlotte," Ashley whispered.

"Lights, camera, action!" I whispered back.

Ashley flipped open the book on show horses Tina loaned us. She was careful to touch only the very edges of the cover.

I leaned close to her. "That horse looks sort of like *Magic*, don't you think?" I asked loudly.

"You're right. It does look sort of like *Magic*," Ashley agreed just as loudly.

I peeked over at Charlotte. I could tell she was listening.

"But you know what?" I asked. "I think this horse is even prettier than Magic. And this horse comes all the way from Arabia."

I bit my lip to keep from giggling.

"Oh, Arabia," Ashley said. "That's where the very *best* horses are from."

"Yeah," I agreed. "This horse must be much better than Magic."

Charlotte charged over. "Let me see that!" she cried. She grabbed the book away from me.

Gotcha! I thought.

Charlotte frowned as she studied the picture in the book. "Magic is a million times better than this horse," she snapped.

Charlotte tossed the book down on the bale of hay and stomped away.

I carefully picked the book up by the edges. Then Ashley and I hurried outside.

"Yes!" Ashley called. She punched her fist in the air.

"Thanks for the fingerprints, Charlotte!" I said softly.

We rushed back over to the picnic table. Ashley dusted the book for fingerprints.

I was too excited to help. I couldn't wait to finally have proof against Charlotte.

"Okay," Ashley said. "This sheet of paper has Charlotte's fingerprints. And this sheet has the fingerprints from the saddle we found on Hot Chocolate."

She carefully laid the sheets of paper out

side by side in the center of the table.

I stared back and forth from one sheet of paper to the other.

Wait. Something was wrong.

I checked both sheets of paper again.

I couldn't believe it. The fingerprints didn't match!

12

CAUGHT IN THE ACT

"I can't believe it," I said. I pulled my bike out from behind the shrubs near the barn. "I just can't believe it."

"Can't believe what, Mary-Kate?" a deep voice asked.

I glanced behind me. "Oh, hello, Mr. Templeton," I said. "I was, um, just telling Ashley I can't believe the horse show is really tomorrow."

What could I do? I couldn't tell Mr. Templeton that Ashley and I had spent the day fingerprinting Charlotte!

Mr. Templeton smiled at me. "Don't worry about the show," he said. "You and Hot Chocolate make a great team."

He started to walk away, then he turned back. "Have either of you girls seen my glasses anywhere around?" he asked.

Ashley and I both started to giggle. "They're on your head," Ashley answered.

Mr. Templeton's face turned red. "I'd probably lose my whole head if—"

"Charlie," a blond woman called. She waved to Mr. Templeton. "I wanted to talk to you about having my daughter's birthday party at the stables."

"Be right there," he answered. "Got to go," he said us. "Thanks for finding my glasses."

"Tina's dad is really nice," Ashley said.

"Yeah," I agreed.

We climbed on our bikes and started pedaling for home. "I didn't think this case could get more confusing," I complained. "But it did. We don't even have another suspect to investigate."

Ashley slammed on her brakes. She stopped so fast her bike's tires left a black mark on the street. I stopped and backed my bike up so it was even with hers.

"Mr. Templeton's first name is Charlie!" she cried. "That's what that woman at the stables called him."

"Thanks for the news flash," I said. "Can we keep going? I'm starved."

"Don't you get it?" Ashley demanded. "Charley Templeton. CT."

CT. The initials on the saddle we found on Hot Chocolate.

"No way," I said quickly. I started pedaling again.

Ashley rode up beside me. "I know you really like Mr. Templeton. I do too. But we have to keep an open mind," Ashley said as we biked.

"And he *is* always misplacing things,

remember?" she asked. "Maybe he used the bridle and the saddle blanket and forgot to put them back in the right place."

I sped up. I didn't want to believe that Mr. Templeton could possibly be the person we were looking for.

Ashley sped up too. "Mr. Templeton knows all about horses, right?" she asked.

I didn't answer. But that didn't stop Ashley.

"Since he knows all about horses, he could have taught Hot Chocolate to go over the high jump and to bow, right?"

"I guess," I admitted. "But I just can't believe Mr. Templeton is behind all this."

"Probably not. But we have to be sure," Ashley said. "We have to get Mr. Templeton's fingerprints so we can eliminate him."

I swallowed hard. "You're right, Ashley," I answered. "And you know what that means— we have to sneak into Mr. Templeton's house."

I peered into the Templetons' living room

window an hour later. Mr. Templeton lay flat on his stomach and peered under the sofa. Tina stood on her tiptoes and ran her fingers over the top of the bookshelf.

"It looks like Mr. Templeton lost something again," I whispered.

"Stop leaning so far forward. They're going to see you," Ashley whispered back.

I scooted back against the thick trunk of the oak tree that sat in the middle of the Templetons' front yard. Ashley and I had been perched in the tree for almost half an hour. As soon as Tina and Mr. Templeton left their house, we were going to sneak in and get Mr. Templeton's fingerprints.

"Why won't they leave?" I whispered.

I wanted to get this over with. I knew Mr. Templeton had to be innocent—and I wanted proof.

"They'll have to leave soon," Ashley answered. "The horse show is about to start."

I nodded. The second we got Mr.

Templeton's fingerprints, I would have to race to the barn, change into my riding clothes for the show, and hop on Hot Chocolate. He was ready to go. I had him saddled and brushed, with his mane and tail perfectly braided—thanks to my practice on Ashley.

Ashley grabbed my arm. "Here they come."

I held perfectly still as Mr. Templeton and Tina hurried out the door. They trotted down the porch steps and headed toward the ring.

Ashley and I counted to one hundred. Then we swung out of the tree and rushed up to the Templetons' front door. It was unlocked, so we opened it and slipped inside.

The house was so quiet I could hear each tick of the grandfather clock in the hall. "Where do you think we should get the finger-prints?" Ashley asked. Her voice sounded much too loud.

I tried to think. But I couldn't concentrate. I didn't like being in the Templetons' house when they weren't home.

Thump. Thump. Thump. I heard the sound of boots on the front porch. Ashley and I stared at each other. "Hide!" I whispered.

I ducked into the hall closet and pushed myself behind the row of coats and jackets. I hope Ashley found a good place, too, I thought.

The closet door swung open. I heard a scuffling sound from the shelf above my head.

I peeked throught the row of clothes—and saw Mr. Templeton rummaging through the closet shelf!

"Now, where did I put that camera?" he muttered.

Please find it fast, I thought.

"Oh, there it is," he mumbled. He turned away from the closet.

Whew!

Then I heard something that made my insides freeze. "Mary-Kate, what are you doing in here?" Mr. Templeton boomed.

13

THE TRUTH COMES OUT

My heart gave a hard thump. I opened my mouth to answer Mr. Templeton.

"I, uh, I came in to return a book Tina loaned me," I heard Ashley say.

Mr. Templeton hadn't caught me—he caught Ashley. He just thought Ashley was me. That happens a lot.

"Do you know how late it is?" Mr. Templeton asked. "We have to get going!"

I heard footsteps walking away, and then the front door shutting.

I leaned back against the closet wall. My legs were trembling too hard to hold me up.

Everything is okay, I told myself. Ashley can just pretend to be me for a few minutes while I get Mr. Templeton's fingerprints.

I took a deep breath and tiptoed out of the closet. I don't know why I was tiptoeing. The house was completely empty.

I really wished Ashley was there to help me figure out the very best place to get Mr. Templeton's fingerprints.

I needed something he touched a lot—that Tina *didn't* touch. Maybe his toothbrush, I thought.

But a toothbrush handle was too small to get a good fingerprint from.

I wandered into the living room. I glanced out the window and saw a crowd of people gathered around the ring, waiting for the show to start.

I was too far away to see anybody's faces, but I knew my mom and my dad and Trent and

Lizzie were out there, waiting to cheer me on.

I had to hurry. I had to get those finger-prints. And then I had to get out to the barn and get on Hot Chocolate before the horse show started.

I turned in a slow circle, studying the room. TV. Armchair. Mantel with trophies. Bookshelf with books. Table with telephone.

I could definitely get fingerprints off the books and telephone receiver. There might even be fingerprints on the TV.

But I knew Tina touched those things too. So I wouldn't get just Mr. Templeton's finger-prints.

What would only Mr. Templeton touch?

The trophies!

Tina told me Mr. Templeton wouldn't let anyone touch them—including her.

Perfect! I rushed over to the mantel and carefully picked up one of the trophies.

Wait. I stared at the name engraved on the bottom of the trophy.

This didn't belong to Mr. Templeton!

"Put that down!" a high voice cried.

I spun around. "Tina!" I gasped.

I stared at her. Her eyes were wide and her face was pale.

"Put the trophy down," Tina said.

"It's yours, isn't it?" I asked.

I read the words engraved on the bottom of the trophy. "First prize. Camden Horse Show. Christina Templeton."

I set the trophy down. "Tina is a nickname for Christina, isn't it?"

Tina sighed. "Yes. You're right. The trophy is mine."

"Wait a minute! That means you're CT," I said. "It was your saddle I found on Hot Chocolate. You're the one who has been playing those tricks."

I couldn't believe it. Tina was my friend.

Tina looked confused. "What tricks?" she asked.

"You got Hot Chocolate's feet all muddy.

You moved Hot Chocolate's bridle and his saddle blanket. And then you even hid Hot Chocolate!" I exclaimed.

Tina sank down on the sofa. "I wasn't trying to play tricks. I...I've been riding Hot Chocolate early in the morning, so no one would know. I was so worried about getting caught, that I didn't always have time to put his things back in the right place—or clean his feet."

Tina wrapped her arms around herself. "My dad almost caught me once. I jumped off Hot Chocolate and tied him up behind the house. Then you found him before I could put him back in the barn."

I sat down next to her. "You and your sister almost caught me a couple times," Tina said. "I had to run out of the barn without taking Hot Chocolate's saddle off once."

Tina shook her head. "You almost caught me that time you were up in the hayloft, too."

"You took the ladder away so we wouldn't

see you—then you came back and rescued us," I said. "Is that what happened?"

"Uh-huh," Tina answered. "But I didn't know it was you two up there until I heard you yelling. I thought it was my dad in the hayloft!"

"There's still one thing I don't understand," I said. "Why didn't you want anyone to know you were riding Hot Chocolate?"

"You know what a worrywart my dad is," Tina said. She rearranged the books on the coffee table. Then she started fluffing the sofa pillows.

"He *is* a total worrywart," I said. "But I still don't understand."

Tina stopped fluffing the pillows and looked at me. "Two years ago I was in an accident. I was taking a jump, and I fell."

"Oh, no," I whispered.

"I was in the hospital for almost a month," Tina said. "When I got out, my dad didn't want me to ride anymore. He was afraid I would get hurt."

I nodded. I bet my parents would have felt the same way.

"I...I was afraid, too," Tina admitted. "But I love horses so much. So early one morning I decided to ride Hot Chocolate. He's the most gentle horse in the whole stable."

"You're right," I said.

"I've been riding him every morning since then," Tina said. "I even taught him to go over the high jump."

"And you taught him how to bow!" I exclaimed. Every piece of the mystery was falling into place. It all made sense now.

Tina laughed. "I was tired of listening to Charlotte brag. I wanted to show her Magic wasn't the only horse who could do tricks."

"It was so great the day that Hot Chocolate bowed during riding class!" I said.

Tina glanced out the window. "Hey, we have to go, Ashley. We're going to miss the whole horse show."

"I'm not Ashley. I'm Mary-Kate!" I told her.

"You can't be!" Tina cried.

I frowned. "Why not?"

Tina pointed toward the ring. "If you're Mary-Kate, who is that in the ring riding Hot Chocolate?"

BLUE-RIBBON DETECTIVES

Oh, no! Ashley was riding Hot Chocolate in the horse show!

"Come on!" I exclaimed. "We have to go." We jumped up and raced for the front door.

Tina skidded to a stop by the hall table. She pulled a roll of film out of the top drawer. "This is why I came back. Dad forgot the film!"

I jerked open the front door, and we raced out. We ran down the porch steps. We didn't stop running until we reached the ring.

Ashley and Hot Chocolate trotted toward

the low jump. "Just lean forward and hold on!" I shouted. "You can do it, Ashley."

Hot Chocolate picked up speed.

I crossed my fingers.

Then—whoosh!—Hot Chocolate was over the jump. A huge grin spread across Ashley's face.

"All right!" I shouted. I jumped up and down, clapping and cheering.

"Way to go!" Tina yelled.

Ashley trotted Hot Chocolate over to the line of horses along the side of the ring.

"Now my dad will give out the ribbons for this group," Tina said.

"You all have worked hard—and that means you are all winners," Mr. Templeton announced. He walked down the row and handed every kid a blue ribbon.

Ashley stared at hers as if it were the most beautiful thing she'd ever seen.

Mr. Templeton swung open the gate, and the horses trotted out. Tina and I raced up to

Ashley and helped her dismount.

"You were awesome!" I told her.

"I was so scared," Ashley said. "But I just kept pretending I was you, and doing all the things I've seen you do when you ride. Hot Chocolate did the rest."

Charlotte stomped by, leading Magic. Her lips were turned down in a scowl.

"What's her problem?" Tina asked. "She got a blue ribbon too."

"She probably only likes blue ribbons from England or something," I mumbled.

Ashley laughed. "Did you—" she started to ask. Then she glanced over at Tina and stopped.

"Our case is solved," I told her. I explained everything I learned from Tina.

"You have to tell your dad the truth," Ashley said to Tina. "You're too great with horses to keep it a secret. You trained Hot Chocolate so well, even I looked good."

"I guess I couldn't keep my secret forever.

At least not with twin detectives around." Tina glanced over at her father. "I'll tell him after the show," she promised.

Ashley handed me the blue ribbon. "This should have been yours," she said.

I handed it back. "You deserve it."

"Let's put it on Hot Chocolate's stall door," Ashley suggested.

"Great idea!" I said. I gently patted him on the nose. "Hot Chocolate is definitely a blue-ribbon horse!"

"And you two are first-prize, blue-ribbon detectives," Tina added.

Hi from both of us,

It's no secret that the Trenchcoat Twins love to solve mysteries. And we have even more brand-new mysteries for you to read! Mysteries that no one has ever seen or heard before—mysteries that even surprise us!

We couldn't believe it when the kids at our summer camp told us that the camp was haunted. Then we heard strange howls outside our cabin. And we saw a swing moving back and forth—without anyone in it! Could there really be a g-g-ghost at our camp? We had to find out!

Want to see how it all began? Take a look at the next page—and get a special sneak peek at The *New* Adventures of Mary-Kate and Ashley: The Case Of The Haunted Camp.

See you next time!

Love,

Ashley Olsen & Mary-Kate Olsen

A sneak peek at our next mystery...

The Case Of The Haunted Camp

Sandy made her voice low and spooky as she began her tale. "One summer, many years ago," she said, "a girl came to Camp Big Bear. She loved it here. She loved the activities and sports. She loved the trees and the mountains and the lake. She especially loved swinging on the tire swing. It was her favorite thing to do."

I grabbed Ashley's arm and held on tight.

"It's just a story, Mary-Kate," Ashley told me.

"She loved the tire swing a little too much." Sandy continued. "The camper left her bunk in Cabin Seven late, late one night to go swinging. Her bunkmates tried to stop her. They said it was too dangerous—a wolf might come down from the mountains, or maybe even a bear. But the camper didn't listen. She ignored their warnings."

Sandy paused and took a sip of her soda. I held my breath.

"And that camper...that camper was never seen again!" Sandy whispered.

I gasped.

"From that day forward, nobody liked to stay in Cabin Seven. Anytime someone did, strange things happened around camp. Arts and crafts projects were destroyed. The volleyball nets were ripped to shreds. Sleeping bags were stuffed with leaves and bugs."

My half-eaten hot dog slipped out of my fingers and fell into the dirt.

"About ten years ago," Sandy continued, "we stopped using Cabin Seven. And the strange things stopped happening." She leaned closer to the fire. The flames threw spooky shadows on her face.

"But to this day, some people claim that they hear the sound of the tire swing creaking late, late at night. And when they look outside—there's no one there!"

I shivered. "Do you think the story is true?" I asked Ashley.

The party can't start without you...

YOU'RE INVITED TO MARY-KATE & ASHLEY'S™

with a shiny dolphin necklace!

with a beautiful keepsake locket!

with a twin hearts necklace!

with a snowflake necklace!

You've watched the videos, now read all the books! Order today!

☐ BCG93843-6 *You're Invited to Mary-Kate & Ashley's Sleepover Party* $12.95

☐ BCG88012-8 *You're Invited to Mary-Kate & Ashley's Hawaiian Beach Party* $12.95

☐ BCG76958-8 *You're Invited to Mary-Kate & Ashley's Christmas Party* $12.95

☐ BCG22593-6 *You're Invited to Mary-Kate & Ashley's Birthday Party* $12.95

Here's a message from Mary-Kate and Ashley...See you at the bookstore!

Available wherever you buy books, or use this order form

- -

Scholastic Inc., P.O. Box 7502, 2931 East McCarty Street, Jefferson City, MO 65102

Please send me the books I have checked above. I am enclosing $_____ (please add $2.00 to cover shipping and handling). Send check or money order—no cash or C.O.D.s please.

Name_____ **Birthdate**_____

Address_____

City_____ **State/Zip** _____

Please allow four to six weeks for delivery. Offer good in U.S. only. Sorry, mail orders are not available to residents of Canada. Prices subject to change.

 DUALSTAR PUBLICATIONS   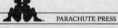   PARACHUTE PRESS

SCHOLASTIC   YIT298

Mary-Kate & Ashley
Ready for Fun and Adventure? Read All Our Books!

THE NEW ADVENTURES OF MARY-KATE & ASHLEY™

ORIGINAL MYSTERIES

- ❑ BBO29542-X The Case Of The Ballet Bandit $3.99
- ❑ BBO29307-9 The Case Of The 202 Clues...$3.99

THE ADVENTURES OF MARY-KATE & ASHLEY™

VIDEO TIE-INS!

- ❑ BBO86369-X The Case Of The Sea World Adventure..$3.99
- ❑ BBO86370-3 The Case Of The Mystery Cruise..$3.99
- ❑ BBO86231-6 The Case Of The Funhouse Mystery $3.99
- ❑ BBO88008-X The Case Of The U.S. Space Camp Mission...$3.99
- ❑ BBO88009-8 The Case Of The Christmas Caper $3.99
- ❑ BBO88010-1 The Case Of The Shark Encounter $3.99
- ❑ BBO88013-6 The Case Of The Hotel Who-Done-It $3.99
- ❑ BBO88014-4 The Case Of The Volcano Mystery..$3.99
- ❑ BBO88015-2 The Case Of The U.S. Navy Adventure $3.99
- ❑ BBO88016-0 The Case Of Thorn Mansion $3.99

YOU'RE INVITED TO MARY-KATE & ASHLEY'S™

KEEPSAKE BOOKS!

- ❑ BBO76958-8 You're Invited to Mary-Kate & Ashley's Christmas Party $12.95
- ❑ BBO88012-8 You're Invited to Mary-Kate & Ashley's Hawaiian Beach Party $12.95
- ❑ BBO88007-1 You're Invited to Mary-Kate & Ashley's Sleepover Party $12.95
- ❑ BBO22593-6 You're Invited to Mary-Kate & Ashley's Birthday Party $12.95

Available wherever you buy books, or use this order form
SCHOLASTIC INC., P.O. Box 7502, 2931 East McCarty Street, Jefferson City, MO 65102

Please send me the books I have checked above. I am enclosing $_____ (please add $2.00 to cover shipping and handling). Send check or money order—no cash or C.O.D.s please.

Name _____

Address_____

City_____ State/Zip_____

Please allow four to six weeks for delivery. Offer good in the U.S.A. only. Sorry, mail orders are not available to residents of Canada. Prices subject to change.

Listen To Us!

You're Invited to Mary-Kate & Ashley's™
Sleepover Party™
-Featuring 14 Great Songs-
Mary-Kate & Ashley's Newest Cassette and CD
Available Now Wherever Music is Sold

The Adventures of MARY-KATE & ASHLEY™

Look for the best-selling detective home video episodes.

The Case Of The Volcano Adventure™

The Case Of The U.S. Navy Mystery™

The Case Of The Hotel Who•Done•It™

The Case Of The Shark Encounter™

The Case Of The U.S. Space Camp® Mission™

The Case Of The Fun House Mystery™

The Case Of The Christmas Caper™

The Case Of The Sea World® Adventure™

The Case Of The Mystery Cruise™

The Case Of The Logical i Ranch™

The Case Of Thorn Mansion™

Join the fun!

You're Invited To Mary-Kate & Ashley's™ Camp Out Party™ *NEW*

You're Invited To Mary-Kate & Ashley's™ Ballet Party™ *NEW*

You're Invited To Mary-Kate & Ashley's™ Birthday Party™

You're Invited To Mary-Kate & Ashley's™ Christmas Party™

You're Invited To Mary-Kate & Ashley's™ Sleepover Party™

You're Invited To Mary-Kate & Ashley's™ Hawaiian Beach Party™

And also available:

Mary-Kate and Ashley Olsen: Our Music Video™

Mary-Kate and Ashley Olsen: Our First Video™

DUALSTAR VIDEO

Join the Party!

Collect all three new videos from Mary-Kate & Ashley.

DUALSTAR
VIDEO

KidVision
A DIVISION OF
WARNERVISION
ENTERTAINMENT

It doesn't matter if you live around the corner...
or around the world...
If you are a fan of Mary-Kate and Ashley Olsen,
you should be a member of

MARY-KATE + ASHLEY'S FUN CLUB™

Here's what you get:
Our Funzine™
An autographed color photo
Two black & white individual photos
A full size color poster
An official **Fun Club**™ membership card
A **Fun Club**™ school folder
Two special **Fun Club**™ surprises
A holiday card
Fun Club™ collectibles catalog
Plus a **Fun Club**™ box to keep everything in

To join Mary-Kate + Ashley's Fun Club™, fill out the form
below and send it along with

U.S. Residents – $17.00
Canadian Residents – $22 U.S. Funds
International Residents – $27 U.S. Funds

MARY-KATE + ASHLEY'S FUN CLUB™
859 HOLLYWOOD WAY, SUITE 275
BURBANK, CA 91505

NAME:_____

ADDRESS:_____

CITY:_____STATE:_____ZIP:_____

PHONE: (____) _____BIRTHDATE:_____